T5-AFS-990

I WAS BORN TO BE A BROTHER

I Was Born to Be a BROTHER

By Zaydek G. Michels-Gualtieri

Illustrated by Daniel Liegey

2003
Platypus Media, LLC
Washington DC USA

Available in this series:
I Was Born to Be a Sister, with story and music CD, by Akaela S. Michels-Gualtieri
I Was Born to Be a Brother, with story and music CD, by Zaydek G. Michels-Gualtieri

Activity Guide available at PlatypusMedia.com

Library of Congress Cataloging in Publication Data
Michels-Gualtieri, Zaydek G., 1992-
I was born to be a brother / by Zaydek G. Michels-Gualtieri; illustrated by Daniel Liegey
p. cm.   Summary: A boy who is "born to be a brother" describes how he likes to teach his sister
what he knows and how, though he sometimes loses patience with her, he realizes that she is
the "best sister in the whole wide world."
ISBN 1-930775-10-5

1. Children's writings. [1. Brothers and sisters—Fiction. 2. Children's writings.]
I. Liegey, Daniel, ill. II. Title.
PZ7.M581851Iw 2003 [E]—dc21   2003048267

Platypus Media is committed to the promotion and protection of breastfeeding.
We donate six percent of our profits to breastfeeding organizations.

Platypus Media, LLC
627 A Street, NE
Washington, DC 20002
PlatypusMedia.com

10 9 8 7 6 5 4 3 2 1

Series editor: Ellen E.M. Roberts, Where Books Begin, New York, NY
Project editor: Gale Pryor, Belmont, MA
Project management: Maureen Graney, Washington, DC
Book design: Andrew Barthelmes, Peekskill, NY
Production consultant: Kathy Rosenbloom, New York, NY

I Was Born to Be a Brother, with story and music CD, ISBN: 1-930775-10-5

All rights reserved. No part of this publication may be reproduced or transmitted in any form
or by any means, electronic or mechanical, including photocopy, recording, or any information
storage and retrieval system, without permission in writing from the publisher.

Manufactured in the United States of America

For Akaela and Miralah—
my way cool sisters!

Some boys were born to be basketball players.

Some boys were born to be scientists.

I was born to be a brother.

Brothers should know a lot of stuff—and I do!

I know how to wind up an airplane and send it high into the sky.

I know how to pump and pull on the tire swing
so it goes around and around really fast.

I know how to set the table for dinner. I put out the plates and forks and glasses. I used to set three places. Now I set four, because my baby sister is old enough to sit at the table with us.

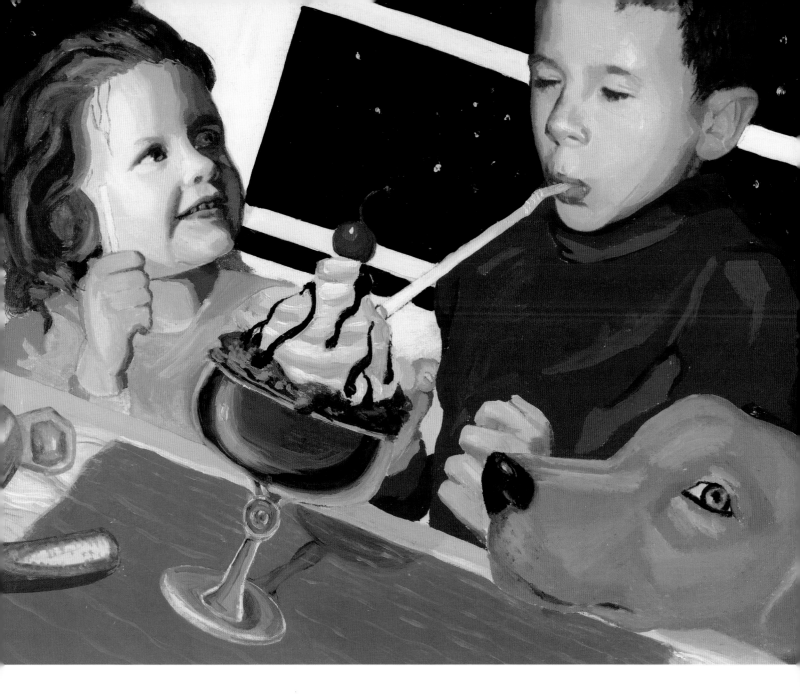

Because I know so much, it is my job to teach my sister things.

Like how to eat ice cream with a straw.

Thanks to me, she knows which sounds go
with which toys.

I explain that even though her teeth have finally grown in, they're just going to fall out. "But don't worry," I assure her, "you'll get more later."

My baby sister would get into mega-trouble if it weren't for me. When we're in an elevator, I teach her which buttons are the number buttons and which one calls the fire department.

She loves to pet the cat. I have to show her
how to be gentle so she won't get scratched.

Sometimes my sister grabs the grown-up scissors.
I make sure she doesn't get them.

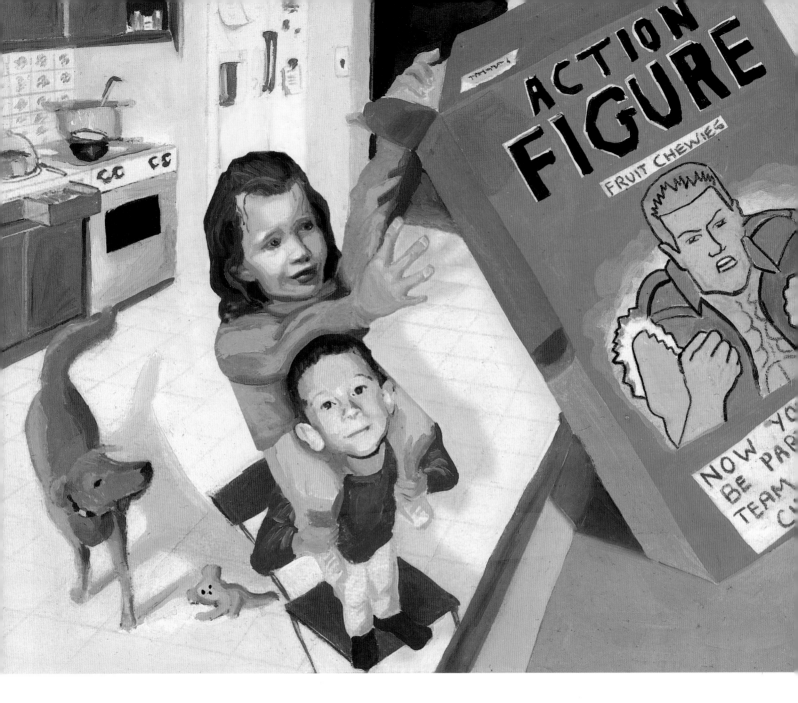

Having a baby sister can be very useful.
When I need to get something from the top
shelf, I just give her a ride on my shoulders.

I can always get her to bring me the remote
when I'm watching cartoons.

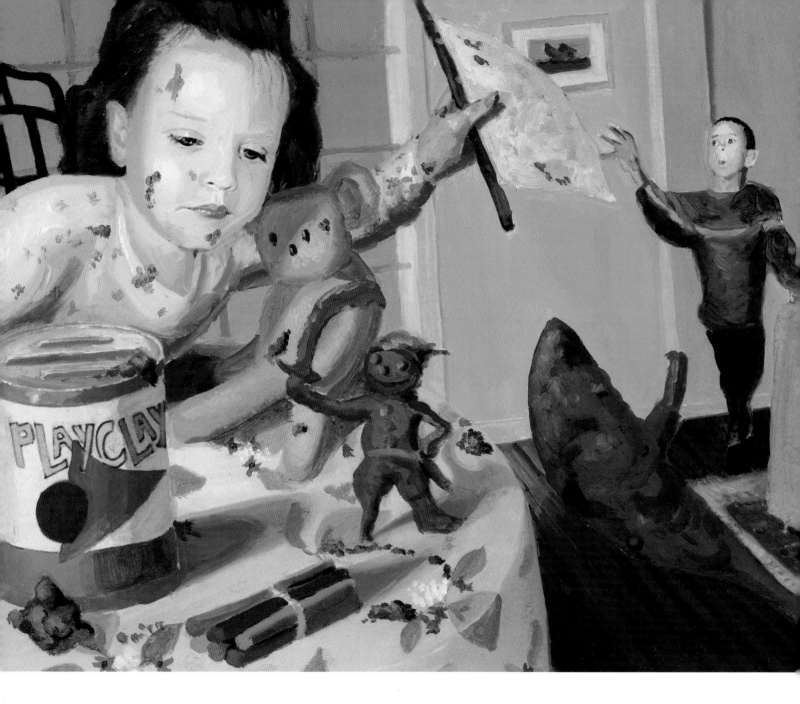

Sometimes when my sister tries to help, she's actually not helpful at all.

When I make things with clay, she makes a big mess.

She tried to help by feeding my fish, but she doesn't know when to stop.

She was really, really not helpful when I spent all day building a racetrack for my cars. I let her race one car—and she wrecked the whole track.

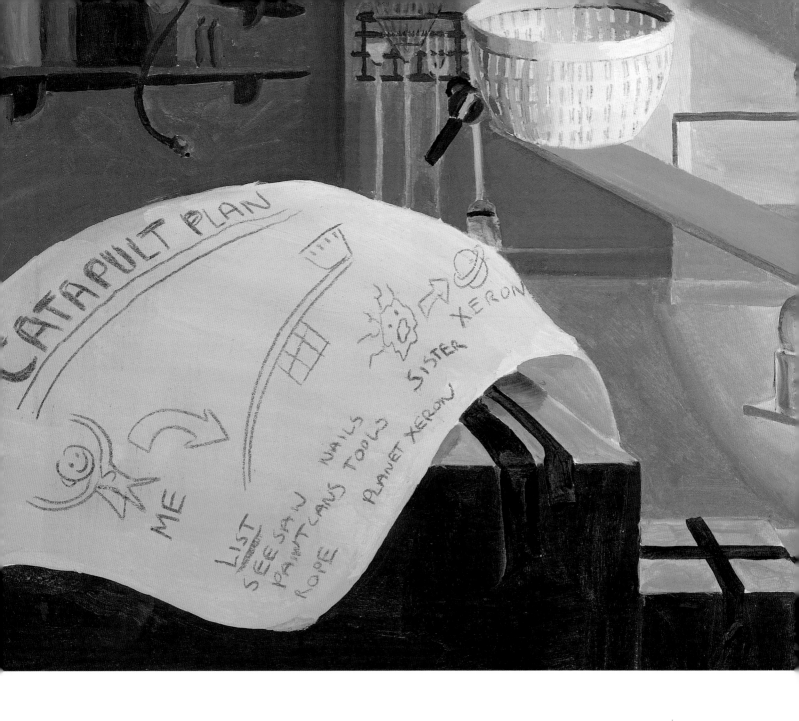

One day, I got so mad at my baby sister, I built a human catapult. I was going to put her in it and send her to planet Xeron.

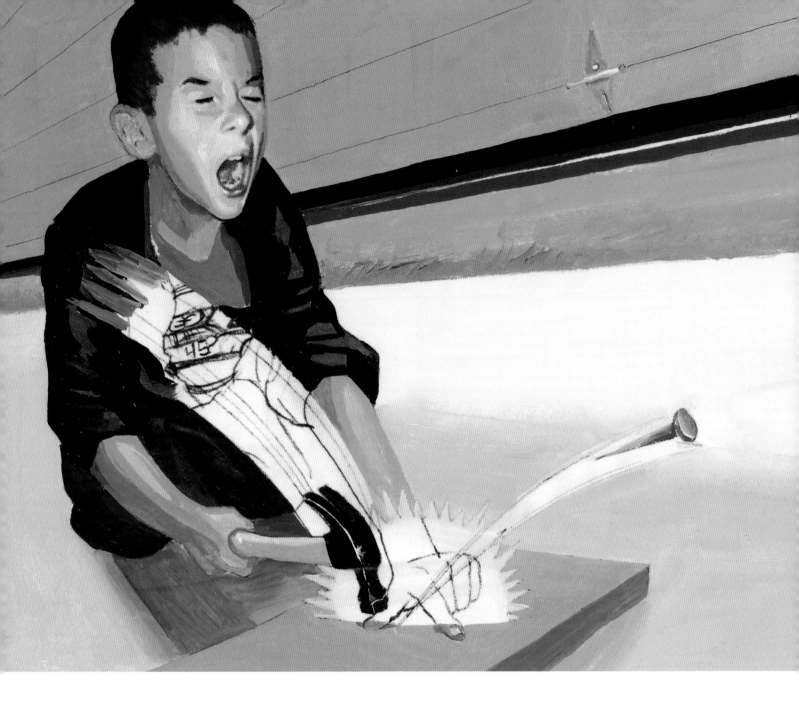

But then, I hammered my thumb. It hurt.

It hurt a lot. I even cried.

My baby sister brought me a tissue, helped me put
a band-aid on my thumb and gave me a big hug.
I hugged her back and I didn't hurt any more.

I think she's the best sister in the whole wide world.

That means I'm the best brother in the whole wide world.